Sadie and Ori and the Blue Blanket

Mother then daughter, will each take our place.

May we do so first with compassion, and later, with grace.

For Mom, with love. — J.F.

Kar-Ben Publishing
A division of Lerner Publishing Group, Inc.
241 First Avenue North
Minneapolis, MN 55401 USA
1-800-4-KARBEN

Website address: www.karben.com

Library of Congress Cataloging-in-Publication Data

Korngold, Jamie S.
    Sadie and Ori and the blue blanket / by Jamie Korngold ; illustrated by Julie Fortenberry.
        pages   cm
    Summary: When Sadie and Ori are born, Grandma knits them a soft blue Together Blanket, but as Grandma gets older, the activities they can do together change.
    ISBN: 978-1-4677-1191-3 (lib. bdg. : alk. paper)
    [1. Grandmothers—Fiction. 2. Old age—Fiction. 3. Aging—Fiction. 4. Blankets—Fiction. 5. Jews—United States—Fiction.] I. Fortenberry, Julie, 1956- illustrator. II. Title.
    PZ7.K83749Sab 2015
    [E]—dc23   2014028811

Manufactured in the United States of America
1 – VP – 7/15/14

Sadie and Ori and the Blue Blanket

By Jamie Korngold

illustrated by Julie Fortenberry

KAR-BEN
PUBLISHING

When Sadie was born, Grandma knit her a soft blue blanket, the color of the sky. Grandma called it their **Together Blanket**, because it was big enough to cover them both.

Grandma cradled baby Sadie and rocked her to sleep in the large oak rocking chair.

That year at Passover, there was a new place at Grandma's seder table for Baby Sadie—right next to Grandma.

Sadie grew quickly.

When the snows of Hanukkah covered the yard, Grandma helped Sadie build a snowman.

On Purim, Sadie helped Grandma bake
hamantaschen and deliver them to friends.

When Ori was born, Grandma made the soft blue blanket big enough to cover all three of them. Sadie told the baby that it was their special **Together Blanket.**

With Sadie snuggled by her side, Grandma cradled Baby Ori in her arms and read them stories.

That year for Passover, there was a new place at Grandma's seder table for Baby Ori—on Grandma's other side.

Grandma spent hours on the floor with them, building grand cities out of wooden blocks, and playing with dolls dressed in doll clothes she had made.

As Sadie and Ori grew, Grandma taught them how to catch a ball and swing a bat.

She bought them red tricycles with orange streamers on the handle bars, and ran alongside them as they pedaled down the sidewalk.

In autumn, Sadie and Ori helped Grandma decorate the sukkah.
When they were done, they drank peach tea under the branches.

In winter, by the light of the Hanukkah menorah,
Grandma taught Sadie and Ori how to spin the dreidel.

When spring arrived, Grandma prepared for the Passover feast. She taught Sadie and Ori the Four Questions.

"You scrub and I'll slice," she said handing them celery and carrots for the soup.

"I'll sing a few words and you sing them back," she instructed.

So Sadie and Ori scrubbed and Grandma sliced,
while they learned the *Mah Nishtanah*, line by line.

The next year Grandma taught them how to make sweet raisin challah for Rosh Hashanah.

Sadie measured the flour and added the yeast.

Ori cracked the eggs.

Sadie kneaded the dough.

Ori stirred in the raisins.

Together, they braided.

While the challah baked, Grandma, helped them
build a tent from their **Together Blanket**.

As the seasons changed and Sadie and Ori grew bigger, they were able
to do more and more. But somehow Grandma could do less and less.

Now Sadie could ride a bike faster than Grandma could run beside her.
Ori could throw a ball higher than Grandma could catch it.

"Why can't you play with us like you used to?" Ori asked.

"There are lots of things I can't do so well anymore," Grandma explained. "That is part of growing older. I can still sit down on the floor, but I can't get back up," she laughed.

"Can you still read stories to us?" asked Ori.

"Of course," said Grandma. And they cuddled under the **Together Blanket** as she read to them.

That year it was too difficult for Grandma to cook the seder meal,
so Sadie and Ori's parents and aunts and uncles prepared the food.
Ori and Sadie helped Grandma set the table.

Sadie and Ori grew bigger still. Sadie could name each state and its capital. Ori could recite the solar system's planets in order.

But though Sadie and Ori could remember more and more, Grandma could remember less and less. Just as her arms were not strong enough to throw a ball, and her eyes were not strong enough to read a book, her mind was not strong enough to remember places or names. That year the Passover seder was moved to Sadie and Ori's house.

"I miss how we used to cook with Grandma and build a tent with Grandma and ride bikes with Grandma," Ori said.

"I miss how Grandma used to be, too," said Sadie. "She always took care of us but now maybe it's our turn to take care of her. And I know something we can still do together!"

So while the soup simmered and the brisket baked, Sadie and Ori gently helped Grandma into the large oak rocking chair.

They squeezed in beside her, one on each side. As they rocked back and forth, snug beneath the soft, blue blanket, Grandma listened as Sadie and Ori read her their favorite stories.

Rabbi Jamie S. Korngold received ordination from the Hebrew Union College-Jewish Institute of Religion and is the founder and spiritual leader of the Adventure Rabbi Program. She has served as a congregational rabbi in the U.S. and Canada, a street musician in Japan, a cook on a boat in Alaska helping with the Exxon Valdez oil spill clean-up, and an Outward Bound guide. She is the author of Kar-Ben's "**Sadie & Ori**" series, which includes **Sadie's Sukkah Breakfast**, **Sadie and the Big Mountain**, **Sadie and the Almost Marvelous Menorah**, **Sadie's Lag Ba'Omer Mystery**, **Sadie, Ori, and Nuggles Go to Camp**, and the best-selling adult titles **God in the Wilderness** and **The God Upgrade**. She lives in Boulder, Colorado.

Julie Fortenberry is an abstract painter and a children's book illustrator. She has a Master's Degree in Fine Arts from Hunter College in New York. Her children's books include Kar-Ben's "**Sadie & Ori**" series and other titles. She lives in Chatham County, North Carolina.